GLOSARIO
GLOSSARY

Azúcar: Sugar

Claro: Of course

Familia: Family

Gracias: Thank you

Harina: Flour

Hola: Hello

Recetas: Recipes

Señora: Ms.

Sí: Yes

Tengo: I have

Vecina: Neighbor

To my Mami y Papi, Emilia and Tomas, for letting me figure things out on my own and making my life the sweetest

Text and illustrations copyright © 2025 by Jenny Alvarado
This book is being published simultaneously in Spanish as *Los viernes comemos churros*.
All Rights Reserved
HOLIDAY HOUSE is registered in the U.S. Patent and Trademark Office.
Printed and bound in January 2025 at C&C Offset, Shenzhen, China.
The artwork was created with digital tools.
www.holidayhouse.com
First Edition
1 3 5 7 9 10 8 6 4 2

Library of Congress Cataloging-in-Publication Data is available.

ISBN: 978-0-8234-5833-2 (hardcover)
ISBN: 978-0-8234-5834-9 (Spanish hardcover)

EU Authorized Representative: HackettFlynn Ltd., 36 Cloch Choirneal, Balrothery, Co. Dublin, K32 C942, Ireland. EU@walkerpublishinggroup.com

FRIDAYS ARE FOR CHURROS

Jenny Alvarado

HOLIDAY HOUSE · NEW YORK

Every Friday, Emi and her Papi made churros for the entire familia.

Emi gathered ingredients as Papi poured oil into the pot.

They made the dough and filled the pastry bag. The oil began to bubble.

PLOP

FIZZ

SPRINKLE

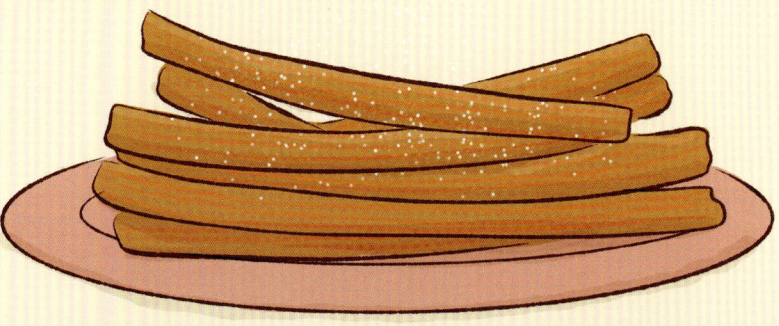

as the familia arrived.

Laughter and chatter filled the air.
It was home.

"FRIDAYS ARE FOR CHURROS!" Emi said.

Until they weren't.

There were many Fridays without family or churros when they moved to the city.

Papi spent a lot of time working—sometimes at his office downtown and sometimes at his office at home.

"Can we make churros today?" Emi asked on the way home from school.

"I have a lot of work today. Another time?" was often Papi's answer.

"Okay, Papi."

The city noise swallowed Emi's words. Emi and Papi walked back to their apartment without a sound.

"¡Hola, Emi!"
Emi broke her silence to greet the only person she knew in their new city, her vecina.
"¡Hola, Señora Luisa!"

A sweet scent swooped out of Luisa's apartment. It reminded Emi of the caramel she and Papi would sometimes dip their churros in.

The smell followed them into their apartment and gave Emi an idea.

"Oh no! We don't have enough flour or sugar, and I can't find the piping tip," she cried.

"I'll ask Señora Luisa!"

Emi bolted out the door without her Papi noticing.

"Hola, Señora Luisa. Do you have flour, sugar, and a piping tip? I'm making churros."

"Hola, Emi. Sí, I have harina. I'll bring it over and help you. You can ask Tomas in 212 for the sugar and tip. He has two daughters around your age."

"Gracias, Señora Luisa," Emi said, sprinting up the stairs.

KNOCK KNOCK KNOCK

"¡Hola, Tomas! I'm Emi from 106. Do you have any sugar and a piping tip? I'm making churros."

"Sí, tengo azúcar. But you can ask Marisol in 512 for the piping tip. She makes very good desserts."

"Thank you, Tomas. Come over for churros, OK?" Emi yelled as she dashed down the hall.

"Wait, the sugar . . ." Tomas called. But Emi was already up the stairs.

"Hi, Marisol. I'm Emi from 106. Do you have a piping tip? I'm making churros."

"Claro, Emi."

Marisol disappeared into her apartment and returned with a box filled with tips that sparkled in the sunlight.

"This one looks just like Papi's," Emi said.

"Would you like to come over for churros?"

"I'd love to. I'll be over in a bit," said Marisol.

"¿EMI?"

Papi's voice echoed from the first floor.

Stopping to quickly invite more neighbors, Emi hurried back to her apartment.

Emi arrived home to find a very worried Papi.

"You can't leave without telling me," he said.

"I wanted to surprise you, but I couldn't find any sugar," Emi explained.
Papi was about to respond when . . .

KNOCK
KNOCK
KNOCK

Smelling of sweet flan, Señora Luisa arrived with flour. And Tomas and his daughters arrived with the sugar.

The other neighbors arrived soon after. Even neighbors she hadn't met came to welcome Emi and Papi to the building.

The scent of sweet dough swirled around as the apartment filled with laughter, chatter, and that familiar feeling of home.

CHURROS

Always cook with a grown-up!

Tools
Piping bags
Star piping tip
Slotted spoon

Ingredients
1 ½ cups water
2 cups all-purpose flour
A pinch of salt
Sugar (and/or any other spices you'd like, such as cinnamon or nutmeg)
Vegetable oil (enough for frying)

1. Bring water to a boil.
2. As you bring the water to a boil, sift and mix your dry ingredients (flour and salt) in a separate bowl. Add other spices.
3. Combine dry ingredients into the boiling water all at once and mix forcefully until the dough is smooth.
4. Remove from heat.
5. As you let the dough cool a bit, bring oil to a slight boil in a separate pan or pot.
6. Place churro dough into a piping bag with a star piping tip.
7. Pipe churro dough into the hot oil and cut at desired length.
8. Fry until golden on all sides.
9. Use a slotted spoon to remove the churros from the oil and transfer onto a paper towel.
10. While still hot, sprinkle sugar over churros or roll churros in sugar or a cinnamon and sugar mixture.
11. Enjoy! Churros are best enjoyed fresh.